10
Minute Tales

The Famous Fireman

When you see these symbols:

Read aloud

Read aloud to
your child.

Read alone

Support your child
as they read alone.

Read along

Read along with
your child.

EGMONT
We bring stories to life

FSC
www.fsc.org
MIX
Paper from
responsible sources
FSC® C018306

Egmont is passionate about helping to preserve the world's remaining ancient forests.
We only use paper from legal and sustainable forest sources.

This book is made from paper certified by the Forestry Stewardship Council® (FSC®),
an organisation dedicated to promoting responsible management of forest resources.
For more information on the FSC®, please visit www.fsc.org. To learn more about
Egmont's sustainable paper policy, please visit www.egmont.co.uk/ethical

Read aloud **Read along**

Elvis was on his way to the Pontypandy Fire Station when he stopped for a chat with Dilys, Trevor and Norman.

"Hello, everyone," Elvis said cheerfully.

"Guess what, Elvis?" said Norman. "Trevor's taking me birdwatching in the forest!"

"Just make sure you're back in time to watch me on TV tonight," Elvis smiled.

Read alone

Elvis stops for a chat on his way to work.
Trevor and Norman are going birdwatching.

Read aloud **Read along**

"The newspaper says that you're singing in a big talent contest," said Dilys, holding it up. "You're going to be a famous superstar, Elvis!"

"Me? A superstar?" he laughed.

But the idea of being famous sounded very good to Elvis! As he went on his way, Elvis daydreamed about singing to big crowds and signing autographs for his fans.

Elvis is singing in a TV contest tonight.
He daydreams of being a famous star.

Read aloud   Read along

At the station, Elvis helped Sam and Penny wash Jupiter the fire engine. Holding his sponge like a microphone, he sang loudly, "La la la laaaaa!"

"Cridlington!" shouted Station Officer Steele as he came into the garage. "Stop that squawking and get on with your work!"

"I'm sorry, sir," smiled Elvis. "I'm just practising for tonight. Dilys thinks I'm going to be famous!"

Elvis practises his singing at the station.
But Steele tells him to get on with his work!

Read alone

"You need to keep your mind on the job," scolded Steele. "Fighting fires is very serious work."

"If I become famous, I may not be a fireman anymore," Elvis said dreamily.

Sam and Penny frowned. They didn't want Elvis to leave the Fire Crew.

Steele shook his head. "You'll always be a fireman first," he said firmly.

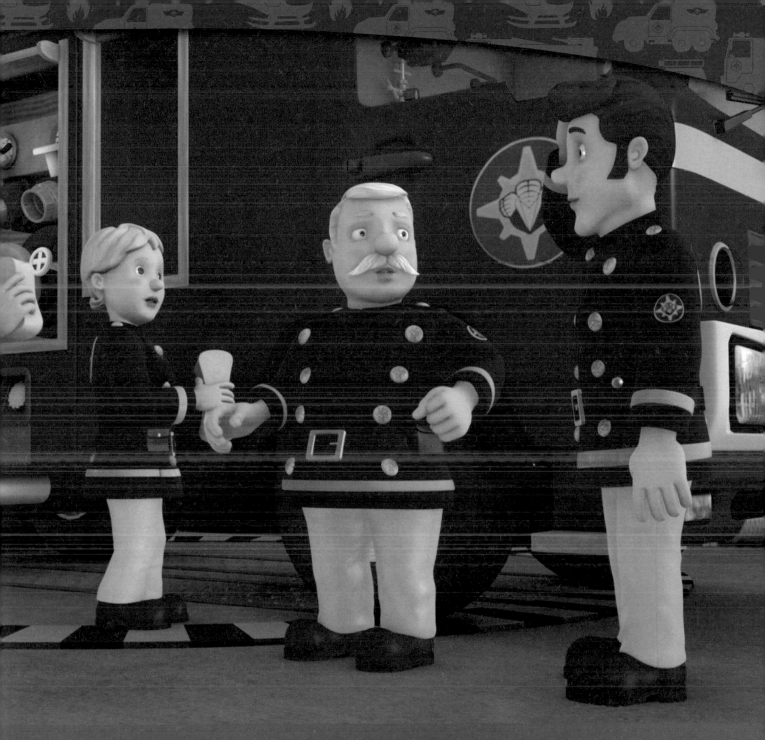

Elvis tells everyone he wants to be famous.
Steele says he will always be a fireman first.

Meanwhile, Trevor and Norman were walking through Pontypandy Forest. Whenever Trevor spotted a bird, he took a picture of it.

"Is it time for lunch yet?" Norman whined. "I'm hungry!"

"Not yet, Norman. We haven't seen half the birds on my list," Trevor told him. "Let's keep going."

Read alone

Trevor and Norman walk in the forest.
They are taking pictures of birds.

Read aloud   Read along

FLASH! Suddenly, a bolt of lightning streaked across the sky.

CRASH! Loud thunder followed a second later, and then it began to rain.

Trevor looked up. "It looks like a bad storm. Time to head home," he said.

As they ran towards the car park, even more lightning crackled down all around them!

Read alone

A lightning storm comes to the forest.
Trevor and Norman run to the car park.

Read aloud

Read along

The car park was on the other side of the forest. But as they got closer to the trees, a lightning bolt hit one and it burst into flames.

"Aaah!" screamed Norman.

The fire leapt quickly from one tree to another. Even the heavy rain didn't stop the flames from spreading. Norman and Trevor would have to find another way to the car park.

"I'll call 999. The fire could destroy the town!" cried Trevor.

The lightning starts a forest fire. Trevor and Norman are scared. They call 999.

Read aloud   Read along

Rrring! Station Officer Steele rang the alarm. Elvis was already on his way to the TV studio, so Sam and Penny jumped in Jupiter and Venus. They raced out of the station towards Pontypandy Forest.

Along the way, Sam spotted Elvis waiting for the bus.

"What's the emergency?" asked Elvis.

"Norman and Trevor are trapped by a forest fire. We're worried it might spread," Sam told him.

Sam and Penny race to the rescue. Sam sees Elvis in town and tells him about the fire.

Read aloud   Read along

Elvis wanted to help fight the fire,
but he would miss his chance to be a star.
He had to make a hard choice.

"I'll come along and help," Elvis decided.
He put his guitar in the back seat and hopped
into Jupiter's cab.

"What about the TV contest?" asked Sam.
"It's your chance to be a famous singer."

Elvis smiled as he put on his seatbelt. "As Officer
Steele said, I'm a fireman first, remember?"

Elvis wants to help, but he would miss the contest. He decides to go and fight the fire.

Read aloud   Read along

Nee Nah! Nee Nah!

Jupiter and Venus sped through the rain with their sirens wailing. When the fire crew reached the forest, they could see the smoke rising up from the trees.

In the woods, Norman cried, "I hear Jupiter's siren!" He and Trevor had tried to find another way out of the forest, but had got lost. They followed the sound to the car park, taking care to avoid the fire.

"I'm glad you two are safe and sound!" said Penny.

Nee Nah! Norman hears Jupiter's siren. He and Trevor follow the sound out of the forest.

Sam and Elvis uncoiled Jupiter's hoses and turned on the strong streams of water. They sprayed the burning trees to keep the fire from spreading towards the town.

Penny aimed Venus' powerful water jet at the fire, too. But all that water still wasn't enough to put the fire out!

Read alone

Jupiter and Venus have water hoses and jets.
Sam, Elvis and Penny use them to fight the fire.

Read aloud   Read along

Officer Steele called Tom at the Mountain Rescue Station and told him about the emergency.

"I'm on it, Sir!" said Tom.

He attached a big bucket to his helicopter, then flew low over the forest lake to fill the bucket with water. He steered Wallaby One above the fire and let the water pour out onto the flames.

Read alone

The fire is too big for the crew.
Tom pours water on it from his helicopter.

Read aloud   Read along

With the fire crew all working together, they finally managed to put out the fire. Pontypandy was safe!

Elvis and Sam put the hoses away as Tom landed Wallaby One in a field nearby.

Sam looked at his watch. "I guess you're too late to get to the TV studio now," he told Elvis.

With Tom's help, the fire goes out.
Sam tells Elvis he is late for the contest.

Read alone

Read aloud   Read along

"**N**ot if you go by helicopter," called Tom. "Jump in, Elvis."

"Wow!" laughed Elvis, as he hopped in next to Tom. "Just like a real superstar!"

"Don't forget this," said Penny, handing him his guitar. "Good luck!"

"Thanks ... I'll be back on duty tomorrow morning!" said Elvis as the helicopter rose into the sky.

Read alone

Tom flies Elvis to the contest in his helicopter.
Elvis says he will be back on duty the next day.

That night, the Pontypandy townspeople gathered in front of the TV at the Wholefish Café. Everyone cheered when Elvis appeared on the screen with his guitar.

"This one's for the best firefighters in the world – Fireman Sam, Penny, and Station Officer Steele," Elvis announced happily before singing:

*I'll sing my songs
Until I burst,
But I never forget
I'm a fireman first!*

Elvis' friends watch him on TV.
He sings that he'll always be a fireman first!

Read alone

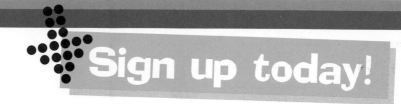
Sign up today!

Monthly Catchup

children's books . mags . eBooks . apps

Does your child love books?

Register for Egmont's monthly e-newsletters and access our wonderful world of characters for **FREE!**

Catchup is packed with sneak previews of new books including much-loved favourites like Mr. Men, Thomas, Ben 10, Fireman Sam and loads more. Plus you'll get **special offers, competitions** and **freebies galore.**

SIGN UP TODAY FOR EXCITING NEWS STRAIGHT TO YOUR INBOX

Head to **egmont.co.uk** to register your details (at the top of the home page) and look out for *Catchup* in your inbox.

Get a whopping **35% off** your first order! So you don't miss out on special offers, freebies and prize, add this email to your address book.

Monthly Catchup
children's books . mags . eBooks . apps

EGMONT

Hello,

You haven't heard from us in a while. It's not because we've forgotten all about you! We've just been working on some brand-new ways to keep you updated about our exciting books. Once a month you can look forward to recieving our newsletter: *Catchup*. It'll be jam-packed with really interesting stuff like, what we've been up to, sneak previews to new books including much-loved favourites like Mr. Men, Thomas, Ben 10 and Fireman Sam, as well as news about brand-new characters and books. You'll also get updates from our magazine team, special offers, competitions and freebies galore.

Stuff to do 'n' win

Signed *Mr. Tickle* to give away...

Thomas the Tank Engine

Zhu-niverse™ here we come!

ZhuZhu Pets® have

Next month...

Sssh don't tell anyone but...

All About Bin Weevils Magazine Launching

All new special *Bin Weevils magazine*, on sale October 5th! It includes 7 amazing free gifts, comics, puzzles, posters, game tips and hints and a lot more.

All About Bin Weevils Magazine Launching

follow on Twitter | forward to a friend

So you don't miss out on special offers, freebies and prize, please add this email to your address book.

E1238